# DIGBY AND THE CONSTRUCTION CREW

# Axel's First Day

**Jodie Parachini**

**illustrated by
John Joven**

Albert Whitman & Company
Chicago, Illinois

A forklift turned up
at the work site today,
with a bright, shiny cab,
full of swagger and sway.

"I'm Axel!" he cried.
"And I'm new in this town!"
He showed off by spinning
in place like a clown.

He zoomed to the left,
then he dashed to the right.
For a truck he was lacking
a built-in brake light!

He didn't know where
on the site to begin.
Yet rather than asking,
he hurtled right in!

He tried helping Gaby
as she lowered her strap,
but his blades were too sharp,
and the cable went...

SNAP!

He tried helping Lori
by mixing cement.
But he spun in a circle
and caused a huge...

DENT!

He tried helping Bruno
by bearing his load,

but his forks dropped the rubble—

**kersplat!** —in the road.

When Axel tried digging
while whizzing around,
he lifted poor Digby
clear off of the ground!

"I'm dizzy!" cried Digby,
and the foreman yelled, "Halt!"

The forklift looked saddened.
"This mess is my fault!"

He moaned and said, "Sorry!
I made such a muddle."

The trucks came together
to form a truck huddle.

"You're nervous," said Digby.
"All new trucks are scared
to start a new job,
and they feel unprepared."

"When Morris was young,
he got into a scrape.
Road rollers don't work
when they're bent out of shape!"

"And I was so anxious
to follow the rules
that I splintered my cargo
and leaked all my fuels!"

"When I," Digby whispered,
"would break things by chance,
I'd fidget and worry,
then do a...break dance!"

"So let's work together.
We'll teach you new skills.
It helps to have friends
who have been through the drills."

The trucks taught young Axel
the rules of the site.

About lifting.
And loading.
And doing things right.

So now when he feels
all his thoughts go awry,

Axel takes a deep breath,
knowing friends are nearby.

He's slow and he's cautious
and gets his work done.
At the end of the day...
Zoom! Dash! Time for fun!

The party begins
as the workday winds down,
with Digby and crew,
plus the new kid in town!

For everyone who has ever felt like the new kid in town.—JP
To my wife, Ana. Thank you for letting me build this amazing life with you.—JJ

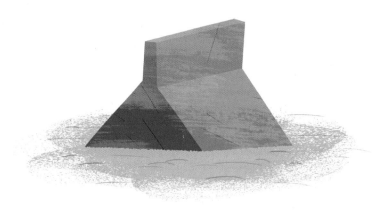

Library of Congress Cataloging-in-Publication data
is on file with the publisher.
Text copyright © 2022 by Jodie Parachini
Illustrations copyright © 2022 by Albert Whitman & Company
Illustrations by John Joven
First published in the United States of America in 2022 by Albert Whitman & Company
ISBN 978-0-8075-1589-1 (hardcover)
ISBN 978-0-8075-1590-7 (ebook)
Printed in China
10 9 8 7 6 5 4 3 2 1 WKT 26 25 24 23 22

Design by Rick DeMonico

For more information about Albert Whitman & Company,
visit our website at www.albertwhitman.com.